# The Lit
# of Shagging

# By Roger A Brown

## DISCLAIMER AND TERMS OF USE AGREEMENT

The Author, Editor and Publisher of this book, and the accompanying materials, have used their best efforts in preparing this book. The author and publisher make no representation or warranties with respect to the accuracy, applicability, fitness, or completeness of the contents of this book. The information contained in this book is strictly for educational purposes.

Therefore, if you wish to apply ideas contained in this book, you are taking full responsibility for your actions.

The Author, Editor and Publisher disclaim any warranties (express or implied), merchantability, or fitness for any particular purpose. The author and publisher shall in no event be held liable to any party for any direct, indirect, punitive, special, incidental or other consequential damages arising directly or indirectly from any use of this material, which is provided "as is", and without warranties.

As always, the advice of a competent legal, tax, accounting, medical or other appropriate professional should be sought.

The Author, Editor and Publisher do not warrant the performance, effectiveness or applicability of any sites listed or linked to in this book.

All links are for information purposes only and are not warranted for content, accuracy or any other implied or explicit purpose.

This book is © copyrighted by Simon 'Amazing' Clarke. No part of this may be copied, or changed in any format, sold, or used in any way other than what is outlined within this book under any circumstances.

# Introduction

Her glistening leg lips were mere inches from my face. Her well shaven pubis mons was as smooth as a babies bum. She laid there, her breathing quickened as she knew what I was about to do for her. There was a shiver through her legs as anticipation rippled through her.

I parted her lips with my fingers, I could see all the way from here throbbing enlarged clit right to her soft wet pussy tunnel and the pleasures that it held for me.

Really, you think I am going to give you all of a great story on the first page, you need to buy the whole book to get to the really juicy stories.

With the in depth sex stories that I am writing in this book it should be immediately obvious that my real name in not Roger Brown. I did actually know a Roger Brown once, but that is not the reason why I chose Roger A Brown for my pen name for this book, it is a play on word. Rogering is another name for shagging or fucking. To give a woman a good Rogering is to give her a damned good seeing too. Obviously potting the Brown instead of the Pink is not a snooker term (actually it can be used in Snooker) but in this case it's referring to anal sex instead of conventions sex in the pussy. So, getting back to the relevance of my pen name. Roger A

Brown is to have a good Anal sex session, and I've had a few of those.

Gee, that seemed like hard work. Yes, I know you just want to get into the nitty gritty like in the opening paragraph but before I get started there are just a couple of things that I want to mention. All of the names and locations have been changed to protect everyone, including those who are not innocent, although all of the general locations are correct. If any of the stories in the book sound like you with someone, it wasn't me. Well it might have been but we don't want the world to know.

If you like the sound of one of these events and you are a single female between 30 and 50 drop me an email, my addy is at the end of this book. I'm quite happy to meet up and have awesome sex with younger ladies but I feel that mid 50's is about my upper limit. Having said that there is the occasion where I was snogging and shagging a 65 yr. old. You'll have to wait till later on for that story, or you can skip over it if you wish.

All of the stories that you are going to read are true. I have had some fantastic times having great sex with a lot of different women and I want to share it with you in the most graphical way that I can. If you are that way inclined, I'm sure that you will love it.

There are stories of things that I shouldn't have done, I did them, they are true and there is nothing that I can do about it now, but as the stories are interesting, I've included them.

There is one time that I really want to mention first. My girlfriend had been living with me for a while so we were used to having both of us in the bathroom at one time, especially as the house had only one toilet and that was in the bathroom, no separate WC here. Totally un-posh.

This one morning she's got up a bit earlier than me so that she could wash her hair. Anyway, so it was time for me to get up. I wandered into the bathroom to have a piss, have a wash and clean my teeth. There was one problem, as I was having a piss she was bent over the bath, bum up. Oh, one thing I should mention, we always slept naked. I finished pissing, washed my hands then started caressing her bum cheeks. Just touching her like this was getting me so fucking horny. From the sounds that she was making, it was working on her too.

Guys, let me ask you a question, what would you do. Do you leave her to wash her hair, or do you do as Spike says in 'Notting Hill', "can I give her one". Yes, obviously I went to go and get dressed. No, no no. Hell no. I got myself squared up behind her. Put my finger inside her pussy to see if it was wet enough. Oh boy, was she wet already, it was like an instant gush. So I guided the tip of my cock inside her and eased in and out until her juices covered the full length of my cock and I could slip fully in and fully out.

The funny thing was, neither of us really had time for a full on sex session so I just went for it. My rhythm got faster and faster until I came deep inside her.

I pulled out and cleaned us both up. I then apologised because I hadn't brought her to orgasm, which is something that I really like to do. 'Oh don't worry' she said, 'just being taken like that was great'.

So there was something that I learned. I usually like to help a Woman cum first. I also love to give as much oral sex as I can but sometime guys, ladies just love to be taken in a completely different way to normal.

## Chapter One

# Cock and Clit

I have to admit that for this chapter I had several different options but they all looked too wimpy. I wanted something that really got down to the nitty gritty.

There are a couple of things that I want to go through here, obviously by the title of this chapter. But here is one of the most important of my findings.

Men and women have sex they way that they like it. I suppose that's why Gay and Lesbian couples have good sex and the rest of us spend a lot of time experimenting. Not that I have any problem experimenting, that's the best part.

Ok, so here is the important bits. Let's look at guys first. Let's look at old fashioned foreplay. So he sticks his fingers up your pussy, pumps them in and out for a few minutes, by which time he's getting arm ache, which to him means that you must be turned on. Then he jumps on top (missionary or missionary) gets his cock deep inside you and starts pumping away until he comes, then he rolls off, says that was brilliant sex and goes to sleep. And you are neither satisfied nor have you cum. Ladies, how many of you have had this happen?

Firstly, it's not his faults, that's the wiring inside his head and he's not yet had a woman tell him how to do it any better or any different.

So let's reverse the situation. The man is on the bed. You get his cock in your mouth, roll your tongue all around his cock, up and down the shaft around and around and up and down a few times. He's good and hard so you climb on, slide him inside you. Then as you move up and down you do the front to back movement, some side to side, slow, fast and before you know it your cumming.

He's looking at you because he's not cum.

Do you know why both of these situations leave the other one unfulfilled?

Ok, big secret time. Each had sex with the other the way that they like it.

Let's start with the ladies first this time. If you want to give the guy the blow job of his life. Get his cock between your lips, cup his balls in one hand and start a nice steady rhythm in and out (up and down, depending upon position). Don't change anything, keep it steady. When he starts making those pre cum sounds, go a bit faster then, as he starts to tense up go faster still and slightly tighten your hand around his balls. Let him cum in your mouth. Your hands should keep still where they are until he's finished cumming (which can be up to 10 or 15 seconds), then you can slowly massage the last few drops out of him. If you haven't already swallowed his cum, deposit it in a toilet or tissues etc.

Why would you swallow his juice? Because, and I don't know why, but it is a mind blowing experience for a guy.

Guys, number one, if she has just done that for you then you have to do this. She has just done to you what your instincts say that you should do to her. Therefore to get the best out of it for both of you, you need to do to her what her instincts tell her to do to you.

Firstly a geography lesson. Insert your finger into her pussy. Then move your wet finger out of her pussy and up towards where here pubes should be. As you get to the top of the pussy lips you should find a little lumpy bit. You will know when you have found it as when you touch it she will flinch, gasp, moan or something.

Secondly, and this is something that I worked out as a teenager. If you make a woman cum by using your tongue on her clit, you will be given 1, an amazing blow job. 2, amazing sex.

Guy, you need to do to her what only a woman would know how to do it to her. She needs the movement, the licking all over the pussy. For us, it's about making us cum fast, for the woman it's about the amount of time that she is enjoying the sensation.

Help her cum more than once and you have got it made for the rest of the day.

Another important fact that I learned, I was much older when I worked this one out. A single shag is great, nothing better than a one night stand BUT, there is nothing more amazing than getting to know how a woman's (or man's) body responds to the right things. Talking is the key here. You have to tell each other what you like and what just doesn't quite work for you.

Imagine having your cock sucked, or your clit licked, it's sooooo good, but if the other person would just do it slightly differently it would be amazing.

Tell them what to do to make a difference. Do what they tell you to do.

I've licked so many ladies pussies, I love it, but it wasn't until one lady said 'Oh, that is so good, but finger me as well' that I realised how she liked it. I suppose it is like holding a guy's balls when giving a blow job. It turns a great Blow job into a mind blowing one.

Right guys, let's get back to the clit. There are a few important things that you need to know. Apart from the obvious fact that they are all different, just like there owners, there are a few simple things to remember that seem to apply to most women.

Gentle, fast, then really gentle. The easiest way to get a woman going is to get your tongue in there but don't just concentrate on the clit. Remember, women like variety (but always listen to what they tell you, follow direction). Roll your tongue up her pussy then over her clit. Down to the lips, the bit between the lips and, if you can, lick inside her pussy. I've seem to find that it's the variety that they love.

Then there is expectation. Once you have been around several times licking the clit as you go. Do another round and miss the clit, go around a second time. The third time, you do lick it and give it some special attention. The anticipation of what you are going to do builds up inside them and blows their minds.

This 'three' scenario seems to work in loads of different areas. Don't forget, it's all about the variety for them. This doesn't mean that sometimes you can just take her when the opportunity presents itself like I did with my girlfriend.

Ok, back to the clit. You've licked her till she is moaning. Give your mouth a wipe and lie next to her for a cuddle and a snog (you get your cock pumped here). Now get your finger on her clit, rub it up and down, side to side, whichever way she seems to like it. Finger her now and again, this adds in the variety and keeps your finger nice and wet / gooey for the clit. Your now going to take her to orgasm.

Again all ladies are different but as soon as she cums (by which time she should be nearly ripping your cock off) stop your finger moving. Her Clit has just gone super sensitive. Think back to when you were young and you first pulled back your foreskin back, your bell end was really sensitive, well that is what her clit feels like in that moment. Give her a few moments then try touching it. As soon as it is ok, start rubbing slow again and as she responds, speed up again, you may be able to get her to cum again. If she does, great, if not, no worries.

Now you can really start playing. Lick her to orgasm, finger her to orgasm (if she will), climb on top and fuck her to orgasm. I've had a couple of girlfriends (both nymphomaniacs) who would just cum and cum. Once came over 50 times each time we had sex. I was trying to be as inventive as possible with what I was doing to her to get her to come different ways. Go for it, its great fun.

Don't forget to search for the 'G' spot. Where is it, your on your own there. lol

Something happened recently when I found a woman who loved playing with my cock. I don't mean the usual 'give it a pounding to get it hard'. No she just loved rolling her fingers around it. She rubbed me so well that I came in my jeans but she was very content to just roll her hand around it and feel the gooeyness, hardness and warmth of my cock.

She was happy doing that, which was fine with me. She also swallowed my load later so she really is a wonderful lady to spend a sexy evening with.

Obviously I gave her my best in return.

So, enough of the teaching, lets get on with the shagging.

## Chapter Two

## She's got hold of my Dick

Guys, do you remember the first time that a girl had her hands down your trousers for the first time and wrapped her tender fingers around your stiffening Cock? Girls, do you remember the first time that a boy had his hand down your knickers and slid his finger inside your pussy?

I can't remember the first 'first' time, but I do remember one girlfriend when I was eleven having her hand somewhere down there. It wasn't until I was sixteen that I got my fingers inside an actual pussy. Boy are they funny things.

The first time I got my hands properly on a pussy was when I was 17, I thought that I was so old, I thought that I was missing out.

This was back in the 80's when I was first working away from home. I met a local lass and we started dating. We'd go out for a trip in my car and end up somewhere that we could have a quiet kiss and cuddle. Well you know how it is, things moved on after a few dates and she seemed very up for it. She's given me a tug in my jeans and I'd got my fingers wet so the only thing to do was to have sex. Now, question for you, have you ever had sex in a car? I know some people do it in the back seat but I was strictly a front seat man myself. Lower her seat back, give her a chance to get her knickers off, climb over the gear lever with both an erection and a condom in place lower yourself on top. Yes, I know I was crap, but forgive me, it was my first time. She probably guided me inside her then I pushed myself all the way in.

OMG, is that it. There is fuck all too it. I can't feel a damned thing. I started thrusting away and eventually I came. I don't think she got anywhere close to cuming, again forgive me, it was my first time.

Firstly, I think I was expecting more. I don't know if everyone is. Secondly, I think it was a standard Durex and not a featherlite so you don't feel a lot through those.

I was so disappointed. After waiting all this time I thought 'if that is it, I don't know what all of the fuss is about.

I was about to find out with my second girlfriend.

We date for a while longer and had car sex a few more times but it was time for me to leave the area so it was over.

One funny story, about 7 years later I met my boss's wife, guess who she turned out to be, yup, the lady I'd lost my virginity too.

## Chapter Three

# Multiple fucks and flesh on soft flesh

There was something so special about the next lady that I dated. I'm still in contact with her 30 years later but unfortunately I've not been inside her knickers, apart from the six months that we were dating, since then. Lord knows I've tried..

It's funny, every guy who has dated her has not wanted her to leave their life. She is such a lovely lady, and oh so kinky in bed.

We'd met one night at a disco, I did say this was 30 years ago. A few dates later and I we were parked in a dodgy car park somewhere half naked with our bits hanging out. I don't know if the following incident was the first night, or one of the first few, but it is so funny. We'd been out, I'd had a couple of drinks, she'd had several. As I was climbing over to her of the car side for a shag, she leaned forward and put her luscious lips around my stiff cock.

I must just mention that I'd never had a blow job until that point. OMFG, I was in heaven. She only did it for a minute then I continued to climb on and get covered up for the actual shagging part. It was probably because I was actually in love with this lady, but the sex, even with a condom was sooo much better.

The following day we were walking through town, she suddenly stopped and started spitting. I was totally confused. She looked at me and said 'did I really do that? Did I really stick your wang in my mouth'. Yeah, for some reason she called it a Wang. I said something like yes and it was great. She just kept on going eugh and yuk. It was still fucking great.

A few weeks later she'd been on the pill for enough weeks for us to have our first shag without a condom. My parents were great. They knew what teenage boys were like and welcomed our bed partners into their house.

So, one sunny Saturday afternoon we were in my old bedroom, kissing, cuddling, getting naked. She did have a strange idea about foreplay. I wanted to get my fingers and head between her legs but she just preferred to cuddle and kiss. She seemed to get warmed up that way. Well, it did make life easier, not so much messing about.

After a while of this kissing malarkey she just wrapped her legs around me and after a little moving around my cock found her tight wet pussy.

Now, the sex in the car had been great, I was totally in love with this woman (girl really, we were both only 17). The blow job had been brilliant but to slip my teenage sensitive cock into her tight juvenile wet pussy was a total dream.

Also unlike a quick shag in the car there was plenty of room, nice bed covers and time to experiment with bed covers.

Thinking about those sessions that we had. I know what I will be thinking about tonight as I have my evening Wank.

One last story from my wonderful time with her. She was on top of me one afternoon doing a wonderful job of getting me to cum inside her when she asked if I would like to 69. Now, I know I was still only 17, or just about 18 at this stage but I sort of knew what a 69 was.

Follow me on this one. So she was on top of me in the usual 'on top' position. She moved my legs further apart and leaned backwards until her back was flat on the bed.

I think she mistook this position for something else. Perhaps she hadn't looked at the pictures properly, or listened properly to her friends story. Because she might have called it a 69, I'd call it fucking painful way of trying to rip your dick off.

Seriously. A cock is supposed to point upwards, up the pussy. Mine was now pointing at my toes.

I told her politely that I wasn't too keen on that position.

It was such a shame that a few months later we went our different ways, well, we were only just about 18.

## Chapter Four

# Mucky Tarts

I'll have to group this next set of 'ladies' together. I was 18 when I split with my first proper girlfriend. I was devastated but having had awesome sex (by my limited standards then) I was looking to see which pussy I could dip my wick in next.

I got with the lady I was going to marry when I was 20 so this will cover the two year period of 18 to 20.

So here I was young and fit and thin and getting fuck all action.

Here were three women through that time, tassel tits, the barmaid and the married one.

Tasstle tits, she didn't wear tassels when I knew her, apparently a few years later she started doing Ann Summers parties and would strip off part way through the night and have these tassels on her nipples and start swinging them around. What a girl and what a pair of melons she had.

What can I say about shagging her, not a lot? I had a room with a single bed. We'd met at a bar and I think she was just looking for tonight's lay herself.

I snogged her outside, invite her in. Hand in the bra, down the knickers, whip them off slap on the old condom and a five minute bang. You see, by the time I was 19 I was still a crap shag, although to be fair, they all seemed to like snogging me.

Yeah, I haven't got a clue either.

The barmaid was probably the weirdest fuck I've ever had. Usual thing, chatting to them through the night. The bar gets quiet so you talk more. Walk her home stopping for a few snogs. We got back to her parents house and sat in the lounge. She had a little fiddle with me but wasn't too bothered. I did manage to get her knickers off and my dick inside her but she really wasn't too interested. Thinking back now I wonder why she didn't just tell me to bugger off.

I think I was shagging her for about 5 minutes as she was making a shopping list or something. You know the old joke about 'pull my knickers up when you have done' well that was her.

Married lady. Well, this is where this chapter gets interesting, eventually you say.

Where I was staying there was a housing estate and one lady was quite well known for having guys back to her house for a shag after the disco.

It's like the other old saying – what's the difference between a whore and a bitch, a whore will sleep with anyone, a bitch will sleep with everyone, except you.

She kept on telling me I was a nice guy and shagging everyone else, bitch.

This one night, she was in with her friend. For me it was a great day, It was my 20$^{th}$ birthday. All I wanted was a birthday kiss. But like the other lady, her husband was working away.

Lets roll on to two hours later when we are at the Bitches house and me and the married lady are downstairs holding on to each others vital organs.

20 years old with my fingers up the wet pussy of a married lady who was a couple of years older than me. The night couldn't get any better.

'We both know what we want, don't we', she said 'I'm cold, let me wear your jumper and we can have sex'. So let me think about it, you want to borrow my jumper and then we will have sex. I think I actually helped her on with it.

A funny thing happened when she laid on the floor, there was this pussy looking at me, it looked good enough to eat. Yeah, I'd read books and magazines describing what to do, but I'd never had the chance to do it.

My oh my, isn't that an interesting experience the first time you do that and, being the 80's, she had a full rug.

Now for those of you under thirty ish, it was unusual to shave off pubic hair before the start of this century. If you wanted to go down on a woman you had to fully accept that you were going to get a mouth full of hair, the curly whirly ones.

So here I am lined up with my mouth poised to 'eat the beaver' and a thought popped into my head, I haven't really got a clue what to do down here. It's a bit like the old Jasper Carrot sketch about the Mole. It's as funny as fuck, just think of me, 20 years old about to dive in when you listen to it.

I have to admit now that this event was over 20 years ago so some details are a little sketchy, and there was probably alcohol involved earlier in the evening but I do remember getting stuck in the.

Why is it that pussy juice is such a funny taste? As a quick side note, I do know that the flavour of that and male cum can change depending upon what you have been eating and drinking. Have a play around with that one if you want.

Yes, I will get back to this story now. From what I can remember I just got my tongue in there and started having a play around. I kept everything nice and gentle and flicked the clit with the end of my tongue quite a bit.

For a guy who didn't know what he was doing I seemed to be doing ok because after about 5 minutes of her making lovely noises she told me to stop because she wanted to suck me off.

That was quick and easy, I'm on my back as she is turning around and her warm, moist eager lips are all over my cock. Fuck me what a night.

This is when I sort of figured out, give them a good licking, if you can help them to cum, great. If not no worries, she will still really enjoy it. Then you should be in for one of the best blow jobs of your life. It's worked for me time and time again.

After a couple of minutes of giving my shaft a good seeing too. She rolled onto her back again dragging me with her. Her intent was obvious, she wanted me to shag her and to do it right now.

After a good half hour of shagging, and snogging, with a few love bites on the neck too, we were all done.

Here is another little thing that I have found. This lady had done it and I've had it happen to me a couple of times, but you can get such a high from all of the foreplay and shagging that your body goes into the ultimate 'fuck me' mode.

You energy zooms up, your sensitivities increase, your stamina goes into overdrive. I seriously must work out what it is that causes it, I could make millions from teaching / telling people what to do.

## Chapter Five

# Engaged!

19 years old, driving a 5 series BMW with a girlfriend who loved sucking my Dick, how more perfect could my life be?

I agreed to marry her (she'd already bought the ring from Readers Digest!) so I had to say yes, plus it was the start of a great month of shagging.

Oh, she was gorgeous. I was 19 she was 18, or something like that. Worked in a knicker factory and sometimes modelled them for the owners, pervs. I was the luckiest bastard in the world.

My broth and I were on visit to the 'rellies' and he mentioned a pub that was wall to wall fanny. We only bumped into these two when we went into the pub after last orders.

The four of us jumped into my car and drove off somewhere 'quiet'. There were plenty of slurping and squidgy noises going off that night.

Anyway following weekend I was back down, picking her up from her house and we headed off somewhere 'quiet'. I think it was her auntie's. We were upstairs and undressed before I could say 'nice tits'.

It's the only thing these days, I find that I am dating women in their 30's and 40's, and they just don't have the near firm bodies any more. Yes, if you are late teens early 20's I am interested in you. Me, my body is all over the place but I do have all of the right things in the right place to give you all that you could ever want!

We only dated for a few months but she loved shagging as much as I did, plus she knew some tricks that I didn't and was happy to learn a thing or two off me.

It's illegal, and I don't condone it in any way but a BJ while you are driving sure does take your mind off the road. Also I didn't know that you could actually get love bites on your dick but she managed it. Oh, did she, lol.

Then again she loved having her cute tight pussy licked and was up for all sort of positions.

Sadly, one disagreement ends a relationship and without mobiles, texting, email and a myriad of other communication option, the relationship ended.

Still, I was happy I'd got my willy wet with a brunet with awesome tits.

## Chapter Six

# A short interlude

I've got a question for you, both boys and girls, have you ever walked into a bar, checked out the talent and realised that the only seats available are next to someone who is, shall I say, facially challenged. Now here is the crunch question, but before the end of the night you've shagged them?

Yup, I did that too. I've only been picked up a couple of times in a bar and I was watching the drunken level of the lady to see if I had been her ugly duckling who turned into a swan. I think I was once but hey, a shag is a shag.

I think to be honest this one was about a 4 pinter. I'd started talking to her after about 3 but her features certainly changed after that 4$^{th}$ one.

By the time I'd downed my 6$^{th}$ she was awesome and we were snogging away in the bar.

Now, because of my previous statement, the 6 pints, how we got to the following I'm not sure but I remember trying to shag standing up, that didn't work so she got on her back in the car park and I climbed on board.

There were no niceties to this one, it was a pure out and out drunken shag.

What was quite funny, I was just about getting to the vinegar stroke when a car horn sounded on the other side of the pub. 'Oh, that will be my dad' she says. I'm inside her, pumping away and she wants to leave and I'm just about to. Hold on. Ahhhh, you can leave now. One last kiss and she was off.

Wow, what a weird night. But a nice little refreshing shag all the same.

## Chapter Seven

# Oh no, it's the Wife

There was a ring tone that came out a few years ago. A guy at work had it. If his missus phoned him instead of ringing an alarm sounded and this voice said 'warning, warning oh no it's the wife'. I don't know if it is on YouTube. Actually, hold on. Yup, it's on there. Hmm, not as funny as when you hear it at work.

Anyway, 20 years old a few months after my evening of ultimate pleasure with the married lady I met the future Mrs 'Brown'.

All of the signs were there 'Don't bother with this one', 'Find someone better', 'you'll be sorry'. Like I took any notice.

Have you ever tried to have sex with someone who really didn't want to? Yeah, that was her. I think another big clue was when she fell asleep during sex. Now don't laugh. Ok, go on then. Yes, I was fucking her on my little single bed and I realised that she didn't have her eyes closed in ecstasy, they were closed because she was asleep, and she wasn't drunk.

The one good side to her being sound asleep was that it's amazing where you can put your wet cock and she will never notice. It was the best blow job she never gave me but don't tell her.

There was a funny incident, when she didn't fall asleep. We were in her room when there was knock at the door. I must just explain that the job had working away from home involved men and women living in separate buildings.

Anyway, I was stripped naked, she was just about there, when this other lady wanted to come in. As she hurriedly got dressed I got under the bed.

This lady came in and after a while we all started chatting, which is really strange because I was still under the bed. After a while I came half out from under the bed and leaned against the wall, leaving my cock propping up that side of the bed.

'Let's see the size of your cock then' she says. No way, the story, and size, would have been all around the area by the following breakfast. I don't actually remember if I got a shag that night.

They say that if every time you have sex in the first year of your marriage you put a pea in a jar, you will never empty it during the rest of your marriage. I disagree. After we got married my wife was offering sex every single night. I was having the time of my life shagging away in my new double bed with my live in wanking machine.

Bearing in mind that I was still naive at only 21, but after two weeks of this I got bored, I didn't know back then what was required to spice it all up. So I said those fateful words, not tonight dear.

In the following 10 plus years, I don't think we had as many sex sessions as we did in those two weeks.

Having said that I do remember once being on top pounding away when the mother in law came in. Good job she didn't come in a couple of minutes earlier, she would have caught me getting gobbled my the missus.

I'm not saying that our sex life was bad, I didn't always get it Christmas and birthday, and if I did that was it for the year which was a real pisser because Christmas and my birthday are two weeks apart. 50 week is a long time to wait, even for a crap shag.

If I was married to someone now and she turned me down for sex, I think I would probably start having a wank in bed next to them and if they questioned what I was doing I would respond with 'You can join in any time you like'.

Thinks go so bad that I ended up going for a 'Massage'. You remember those days when 'Massage parlours' were beginning to get popular. Well this was about 5 years before that.

I was probably about 29 by then. I had two kids, I think they were both mine, and therefore we had had sex at least twice. But not much in the 5 years since the second one was born. I was climbing the walls, absolutely gagging for it. Guys, you've been there, your cock just feels like it is going to explode if you don't get some pussy action soon. Thanks goodness that today via the power of the internet you can find a willing escort within 5 miles of where you live, to do the services for you.

Well when I set up this visit to a Massage lady, I didn't know what was going to happen.

I walked into this room and there stood this lady, she was probably 20 years older than me. I though ok, nice massage coming up. I paid her the £40 (shows you how long ago this was) and she said strip off and lie on your frond on the bed. I thought, ok, I'm not sure where this is going so I will take me shoes and jumper off and see where we go from there.

After taking my shoes off I stood up and she was just whipping her bra off. Ahh, I thought, I might like this more than expected. I climbed out the rest of my clothes and jumped on the bed, stiffy an all.

I really didn't have a clue what to expect. I would put this lady in her mid 50's, she was a lot older than me but for what I wanted, Human, Female and pulse, were about my only parameters.

She started off by giving me a lovely back massage. As we were talking away I was stroking her leg as she was straddling my back. I thought I would be really cheeky and ask if I could finger her while she was massaging me. I seem to remember asking what area's I could touch and what was ok. The long and short of it was, yes and anywhere. So while her hands were on my back, I found her shaven pussy, the first one that I had ever touched and slid my fingers between her thin pussy lips.

Let's just recap here. I'm married and I've not got a shag of the wife for well over 6 months and here I am, a quick phone call, a short drive, £40 and my fingers are inside this woman's cunt. How awesome is that.

So that she could massage me totally I had to leave her pussy alone but yeah.

She gave me a bit of a front massage and was thinking about giving my cock a tug to get it had but it was stood to full attention.

'Would you like me to give you a blow job'? Yeah, like that is the sort of question my wife asks me. I think in 14 years of marriage I got my dick in her mouth about 6 times.

'Yes please', I'm far too polite. Back then you didn't get a BJ without a rubber, I'm glad all of the girls these days do it without because it really is a waste of time. But on this day I was a horny as fuck. She could have wrapped a newspaper around my dick and I would have still cum after a couple of minutes.

So there she is, her mouth going up and down on my shaft. To increase the sensitivity through the rubber she pulled it tight, yeah, that didn't hurt at all, but I think because it was hurting a little bit, I could actually feel her mouth.

I don't think it was the sensation, I think it was the view. Her tits were flopping all over the place as she was pounding her head up and down on me. Moments later I dutifully filled the condom.

Again, this is something that my missus never used to do, she cleaned me up and played with my dick and balls for a few minutes until I was hard again.

'Would you like me to climb on top so that we can fuck'? I needed to move to be in the same city as this lady, so polite, so ready to please and she would have sex with me.

'Yes please' I said, just fucking climb on and shag me, I was thinking.

She popped another rubber on my dick and climbed on.

There are something in life that I really don't understand but why is it that some pussies are like a bucket and some are oh so wonderfully tight?

My missus had one like a bucket, now I know some of you will be thinking, yes but if she's given birth to a couple of kids then it will be. Ah, but, she had those by caesarean, nothing came down the tube.

This lady, though, she had a pussy as tight as a 16 year old virgin. Ok, so I'm guessing there, I never did have a 16 year old virgin. As a teenager I did get to finger a couple of girls who were virgins but that's as far as I got.

So back to the scene in this dodgy room. Here was this woman, on top of me pounding away. I'd not had sex like this in years. Her tits were swinging in all directions. I seriously did not want this night to end.

I think she was getting a bit of a sweat on, plus the fact that I that I had done fuck all since I got there. 'Would you like to do me doggy', it felt like another half dozen Christmas's and birthdays had all arrived at one.

We repositioned ourselves so I could get in behind her and she popped me inside, rock and roll time. I banged away until I came again.

Did I feel guilty about having sex with another woman instead of my wife? Yes, for about 2 seconds. If a dog gets fed plenty at home, it will never stray (or something like that).

This was August and I'm not sure if I had sex with the wife again that year! That's how bad it was.

I visited I think, three more 'massage parlours' before I finally left the wife. No it wasn't just the lack of sex, well ok, that was probably a lot of it but anyway, you don't want to hear about that.

So, now I am single (technically separated but who worries about technicalities) and free to do what I like with whome I like. That is once I can pin a woman down long enough to shag her.

Now this book is going to get really interesting. You've read, or at least heard of 50 shades of Grey…………

# Chapter Eight

# ……..Well this is nothing like that

This is real life.

Some of the most mind blowing experiences that I have ever had are in this chapter.

This all kicked off just before I left my missus. I'd really had enough. I was mid 30's, prime of my life and I wasn't getting any attention sexual or otherwise when the lady at work who sat next to me, propositioned me.

She suggested that I aught to do a massage course and that she would be one of my first clients. I said I wanted to do massages with both people nude. Yes, she knew this……

I left my wife that weekend and we went for a drink.

Ok guys it's tip time. If you walk into a bar looking for a nymphomaniac, which lady are you going to pick first? The stunner, yeah.

You are so wrong.

You want to go for the most ordinary looking lady you can find. She is probably the one who will be wanting you twenty times a night!

Seriously I've had that and better.

This lady I worked with looked like the sort of lady who :- would never allow a penis near her mouth, never mind in it. Would have sex twice a year. Would lay back, open her legs and think of England.

I am glad that I am so wrong. The only down side was that although I was technically separated. She was married and her husband worked at the same place as us. Awkward doesn't cover it.

I need to give this lady a name. I've picked Mary because it's not her name (well that's obvious) and I don't think it was her middle name either.

I got invited to a badminton game in the evening. There were two other guys me and her. I sort of knew the two guys but god, I just wanted to get my hands on here. Anyway, a quick hour of sweaty badminton later and we were sat in her car.

She was totally the master of tease. You know what it is like when you just want to kiss someone and you can't think of anything else? Well she knew how to keep you going. I think if I had just got out of the car she would have got out and snogged me but while I was sat there, she kept me going. I think that night I eventually got a quick kiss.

The following week, why is it that a week is so long when your cock is throbbing? She's already hinted that she wanted more after the badminton this week. Gee's I couldn't get any hornier. After an extremely long hour of badminton we got down to some base or other in the car.

Apparently she'd had several affairs before and after being married and she had really honed her teasing skills, best of all for me, she really loved it too, so she wanted to teach me so that I could tease her.

Most ladies when they are reaching inside your trousers are wanting to play with all that they find down there. They will play with your bell end, rub your shaft and handle your balls. Oh no, not this one, she just gently stroked the side of my cock. It's not really something that I am into, on me, but I love giving it as most women love it. They love the anticipation.

Guys, follow some of the tips that this Mary passed on to me and you will have women coming back to you time and time again. Regardless of looks etc.

Getting my hand inside her bra to her voluptuous breasts, I had to spell check that word. I started to rummage around the whole breast and worked my way around towards the nipple. I rolled my fingers across it and she gasped. 'Go around it, just around it'. Well, I've always been good at following instructions, so that is what I did. Oh the noises she was making, and we were sat in her car.

Every now and again I would allow my fingers to move a little closer and she would make these wonderful sounds again. Oh I love this game. Another good indicator that I was doing a good job was by how tight she was now squeezing my cock. She'd do the gentle touching thing as I missed the nipple but if I left it a good few seconds, then rolled my finger across it I got a tight grip and a few good tugs on my throbbing organ.

A while later my hand was slipping south to her pussy. I love a good pussy, they get so so wet and this night her's was dripping. I thought, let's be clever here and do to her pussy what she wanted me to do to her nipple. I teased around giving the clit a gentle touch now and again. All the time her hand was down my trousers and I was multitasking kissing her at the same time (it's about the only thing that I can manage to multitask).

A couple of nights later she visited me in my caravan. It wasn't very big but hey, clothes off and away we go. Actually, this night something very special happened to me.

Picture the scene. I'm on my knees and she's on all fours in front of me. My cock is suck well into her mouth. Yeah, she's facing me, not doggy style. Cock in her mouth with one hand on my balls.

I was in absolute heaven, she was taking most of me in and was moving backwards and forwards. Then I got the feeling.

Now I don't usually like to interrupt a woman when she is working, and I don't like interrupting people when they have their mouthful but I was getting ready to explode.

These days it is something that I do like to clear up before hand, do you or don't you swallow?

We had neglected to have that conversation. Actually I don't remember their being any conversation……

I think I gave a warning like 'fuck, I'm going to cum', just in case she wanted to get off but she thrust her mouth deeper and faster onto me.

Well, she is either happy to do this or this relationship will be over .

BOOM I came, it felt like gallons of the stuff.

Ladies, I don't know if you realise what it is life for a guy when he 1, cum's in your mouth. 2, you swallow it. It's like having another orgasm.

There she was licking her lips in front of me. She fucking loved it.

The following day she was off on holiday, as she described it, taking some of me with her.

Hell, we had fun for a few months. She was certainly the master of tease. I would sometimes meet her in the bar where she worked, she would walk past me, ignoring me but as she went past her hand would just touch my crotch.

Wow what a woman.

Shortly afterwards she left her husband and settled down with another woman. I wonder if they do threesomes now, I must try and find her and find out.

## Chapter Nine

# Internet dating

The guys at work used to call this 'care in the community' because of some of the doggy women that I would find.

Me I didn't care. I shagged half of them.

I can't remember which order these came in but let's start off with the aromatherapy lady.

Internet dating for me seems to be 300 messages to different ladies. 30 will chat for a short while, 5 will meet up for a date and I'd have sex with 2 of them. So really it was all about finding lots of women to message and keep on pumping the message out, you get there eventually. Oh, and there was 1 every few that I met that I actually dated for a while.

This one, she was really tall, 6 foot something, and she ate really fast but she was nice enough.

I'd had dinner at her place. She lived in her aromatherapy studio so we had dinner off the side of the aromatherapy bed! Really strange that one.

Here is another little tip. It's something that I use. Just because you are getting on well, don't assume that you are being invited to stay the night.

With this lady, we'd had dinner and shared a bottle of wine. We'd been snogging but hadn't got to the groping part. She asked if I would like more wine, we had plenty between us. I said I'm up to my limit if I'm driving. She looked at me and filled my glass.

I'd said that I wanted to stay, she agreed that she wanted me there.

A bottle or two of wine later and we were in bed naked. It was around this time that she mentioned that she hadn't had sex for 10 years. Really 10 years. She'd been married to this guy for 15 years. I'm sorry, but I would have left years ago. I know marriage is not all about sex but it is about loving and nurturing, and having great sex.

Quick question, you might have heard it before but here we go. What's the difference between shagging and making love?

Shagging is what the guy does while the woman is making love. Naa, it isn't as funny written down and when you're sober.

Anyway, so we are laid there in bed. Clothes are scattered everywhere and were snogging away. 'So' I ask, 'when was the last time that a guy went down on you'? 'I've never had a guy do that to me'. Several thoughts flashed through my mind. The first was aww, bless. The second one was really, never. The third was 'dinner time'.

I repositioned myself between her legs and gave her the best licking that I could. I took my time to get her aroused slowly, I licked her pussy lips, sucking and pulling on them. I flicked my tongue inside her pussy and ran it up to her clit. We had all night but she had an appointment with an orgasm that I wanted her to keep.

She kept it all right and boy was she thankful.

The cock sucking that she gave me after that was to of this world. She took her time too. Sucking on my balls, up and down my shaft, then she started pounding up and down on me with her mouth.

Having not discussed where my 'seed should be sown' I thought I'd better warn her. 'If you keep on doing that, I'm going to cum'. She stopped sucking me but kept on wanking me slowly looked in to my eyes and said 'I thought that is what we were supposed to do' then got back to her awesome job on my cock.

Just as I was about to explode in her mouth, she moved it off my cock and started licking the shaft and side of the head. I got the great explosion that a cum in the mouth gives without her getting what she didn't want. It was an awesome time.

Some more kisses and cuddles and we were both asleep. I repeated her licking in the morning so that she'd actually been licked out twice in her life and she have my cock and balls the awesome treatment again.

The next lady I'll mention had quite a thing for Cider. Take a 4 pack with you and you had sex and a great blow job including your load being swallowed.

I would turn up with 2 four packs. Hey, why not.

One of the guys at work knew of a Cider called Dickens. Which became Dickens Cider, and Dick inside her. Naa, again, not as funny as when you're telling it half cut.

She was a big girl but a nice lass. She didn't half snog well, had a pussy that was lovely to chew on buy boy oh boy could she suck a cock. Especially when you knew that she was going to take your cock deep and take the full load.

Here though something really weird, but great happened. Apparently some women can actually faint after an awesome orgasm. There is a French word for it and it roughly translates into 'the little sleep'. Let me have a look on google.

As if by magic the answer appears, good old Wiki. It's actually 'La petite mort' meaning the little death.

Well in knew ladies could have this happen to them, but I didn't know that something like that could happen to us guys. Well one afternoon after a session of kissing, licking, fucking and sucking I exploded into her mouth and kept on orgasming.

The squirting stopped when my load had been spent but oh my fucking god, it was like my whole body was orgasming at the same time. I'm not sure how long this went on for 30 seconds, maybe longer but super super wow.

I never did work out what happened that day but I need to do more research into it. Any ladies that would like to help me in my research?

## Chapter Ten

# Nymphomaniac

In a book about sex, more correctly, about shagging, there has to be a chapter on nymphomaniacs. Now this lady that I dated on and off for a number of years was I suppose technically not a nymphomaniac, she could actually last a few days without needing a good seeing too.

I suppose I'd better give this one a name too. Let's call her 'swallows a lot', I'll describe later on what her favourite trick was.

I'd actually met her on an internet dating site. It's had been slow to get off, I don't think we actually got into bed for the first two or three months.

We'd slept together, i.e. shared a bed, a few times but not got around to more than kissing even thought I'd rub my hard cock up and down her back lovingly. I'm not too sure why that didn't work.

Apparently we were just being 'good friends'.

Anyway, we'd had some drinks at my house and went to bed. After we had been snogging and playing with each other's joy toys for a while she disappeared under the bed covers and started sucking away on my cock.

She was a large girl with great enormous tits that would just wobble all over my legs as she was moving backwards and forwards and up and down on my cock. She also had a lovely soft mouth. Oh how I miss her mouth.

The next thing I know I'm exploding in her mouth and she is swallowing away like a trouper.

A quick snog and she was back nice and gently on my swollen and throbbing cock. She carried on for another twenty minutes or so until I came again. After that she was on me for another half an hour until I came a third time.

As totally amazing as it was, after an hour I just couldn't take any more. So I decided to give her the same awesome time that I had had from her.

Yes, I did say an hour blow job. Ladies if you want to impress your man, there is a goal to achieve.

There was a lot I learned that night. I learned what it takes for her to cum the first time, how quickly she can cum the second time and how, if you get it just right, you can totally control the orgasms. She must have cum 30 to 40 times in that hour, I'm not joking.

The trick here is to bring the lady to the boil by licking her clit till she cums. Then leave the clit alone but lick all over the pussy until she's calmed down a touch. Then oh so gently back onto the clit, if you are a little too quick the clit will be to sensitive and she will be climbing up the bed away from you. As the clit calms down you can get back onto it again, building steadily until she has a shuddering orgasm again, this can happen within a minute or less. Certainly by the time she's had 10 the whole body is in orgasmic shock and will cum very easily.

Well, she would anyway.

I learned something else too that night. If you kneel down for an hour with your mouth in a ladies pussy the blood flow stops in your legs. I went to get off the bed, my legs didn't work and I fell / rolled off the bed and ended up in my wardrobe. Funny as fuck.

The funny part to this story, I woke up in the morning to find her snuggled next to me, reaching between her legs I put a couple of fingers in her still soaking pussy and snuggled up next to her. She woke up shortly afterwards, realised I was inside her looked at me and commented that it was a funny thing to be doing if we were just friends. She had totally forgotten last night's events.

My hour of licking would seem to have been wasted but at least I'd learned how she came, what she didn't like and what she loved. She was quite surprised how well I knew her body when we finally came to our love making. Naa, she called it shagging too. What a lady.

The biggest problem with this lady is that she was always late. Now I'm not talking stuck in the traffic late. I'm talking about come around to mine for dinner at 7 and she would around just before 9 type of late.

After a few weeks of this waiting in all night for her I got fed up and said I couldn't do it any more, it was over.

A week later she started texting me and asking if we were still friends, yes, of course we are. That weekend she came around for a coffee.

The first half of an hour went well, we were just chatting away. Then she said 'I had this dream about you the other night, we were walking towards each other on the beach and the next second in the dream we were shagging. Oh right I said.

A couple of minutes later she mentioned it again 'it was so vivid, it was like we were there'. Oh right.

She mentioned it a third time. I thought to myself, I'm being really thick here. So I asked her, was it just a dream or are you trying to tell me that you'd like a shag?

'Can we', she said 'you kiss so well and I just need to shag you. Can we'. Yes, of cours..... she nearly dragged me upstairs, I threw my clothes off. The moment she saw my hardening cock she was onto like a deranged sexual deviant. I was trying to get laid down on the bed and she was already sucking away.

She said that sucking cock got her so turned on.

Hell, I was in heaven, lol.

That was a wild, wild afternoon of sex. I have a feeling it was a Sunday so wow, what a way to end the weekend.

We dated and broke up a lot over the next few years but always the sex was amazing. But unfortunately we were just too different to ever be together. Never mind, the break up sex was amazing too.

## Chapter Eleven

# Friends with friends with benefits

Yes, you did read that right. A friend of mine had a girlfriend in Wales, only about 30 miles away from where I was working at the time in Bristol. I was chatting to him one day and I happened to say, it's a pity she hasn't got a friend who I can shag. There is always her sister, she'll shag you, he said.

Really, yeah. I'd met his girlfriend so knew what she was like so I asked what the sister looked like, 'oh', he says, 'she's fucking ugly'. I don't care I said, a shag is a shag.

A few weekends later I met him at his girlfriends and we went over to the sisters. Oh my fucking god, he was right. She was ugly, and boy did she have a gob on her.

He'd said before had that she would do anything for me, suck me and swallow my load. I thought ok, she's rough but a good shag is all that I am after.

We went out for dinner that night, total disaster but when we got back I must have looked like a cross between Brad Pitt and Tom Cruise because she couldn't wait to get me into bed.

I'm not sure but I think the 6 pints that she had might have made me look good.

Yes, 6 pints, she was drinking them faster than me.

We did a bit of shagging that night, from what I can remember but every time I suggested something she said no. Do you Swallow cum, no. Do you at least give a blow job, no. Turn over, lets do it doggy, no.

My mate and his girlfriend in the next room must have been wetting themselves. Straight up missionary was all that she would do.

The following morning she was up and starting to sort out the kitchen for breakfast. My Mate and his girlfriend were rocking the roof beams in their bedroom.

The night before after 5 pints, I was a light weight and couldn't manage the $6^{th}$ one, she still looked ugly but not so bad.

One look at her and I thought I really don't have any standards.

I took my bag out to my car and as I stood there I thought I just cannot go back in there. I got into my car drove 5 miles, parked up and texted my mate. No worries he said, she really is fuglly.

A few years later this same mate set me up with his new girlfriends neighbour. Now she was nice, and up for it.

She was divorced with a couple of kids who were away at their dads for the weekend so she was foot loose, fancy free, and up for a good shagging. Well, I could do some of that.

I don't remember if we had dinner or what but we walked back to her house. I think we had snogged once by this time and it was bed time.

Me being the slut / nympho that I am, I'm quite happy to disrobe in front of a woman. It didn't take her long to get her kit off too.

I don't really know what happened that night. I think we gave each other a good going over with our mouths. I know I can't resist licking a pussy.

Well, something happened that I had never come across before.

I've described previously how I like to lick a pussy. I like to start licking all over, flicking the tip of my tongue all over everything and as the woman warms up I concentrate more and more on the clit till I get her to cum.

Well, with this one, I'd licked the clit twice. Literally, lick lick and she was on her way to orgasm. I tried to get my tongue in there again to give some more but she was already bounding all over the bed.

Bang, she'd cum. Ok, back in the with tongue again. One, two, three, keep the tip of your tongue just about where the clit is and as she bounced up and down orgasm after orgasm I just lay there with my tongue out. She was in absolute heaven.

It was the same with the shagging. A quick 5 thrusts and she was bouncing.

There will be some guys out there who are thinking ' you lucky bastard' and yes you are right but I like to give as much as I get and this seemed all a little one sided. She sucked me for ages and swallowed my load and I licked her for 5 seconds and she came.

Anyway, we both had a great night, and the same again the following morning. At least I actually stopped for breakfast with this one.

The following morning I set off back the 100 plus miles back home when I got a text from my ex. You remember from the previous chapter 'Swallows a lot'. Would I fancy popping in for a 'coffee', that was usually a signal for a shag.

So I laid there getting sucked off by the second lady that day feeling really good about life. 3 great shags by two great women in 2 days. Including 2 on the same day.

## Chapter Twelve

## 1 hour fucks

Should guys pay to have sex with women? Absolutely not. Do I care, do I fuck.

If I could meet women ever month who said 'oh, I could really do with a shag, do you know any guys that would shag me'. I would never have to pay for sex again.

When this book goes viral and I'm selling thousands of books a month, I won't need to pay for sex.

Until then, I do, well have done. Actually yes. Oh, the problem about writing about sex when you are not getting any is you just need a willing woman to be under your desk as you are tapping away just slowly sucking on your shaft, sliding her mouth slowly and rhythmically up and down. Fuck, I've got to make a phone call.

After my first couple of visits to 'massage' parlours as they were back in the 90's, and after my subsequent separation I ended up living in my own place. Here it was a lot easier to phone one of the new 'escort' agencies and have a lady come to your house.

I phoned up this one place. The lovely lady on the phone asked me if I would prefer the Brunette with the perky breasts or the Blonde with the large breasts.

Guys, what is it about us and the Blondes. For me Blonde is best and one with large breasts, oh yeah.

I selected the Blonde. Ok, she said, I'll be there in half an hour. What! You picked the Blonde, that's me. Oh boy, she sounded good too.

I had a quick shower and put on a t-shirt and my jogging pants, no grunts (underwear for the posh ones).

When she arrive, wow, what a lovely lady and yes, she had great breasts.

I paid her, as is customary, and led her upstairs. We kissed, then she got on her knees and went to pull down my joggers. Pow, there was this hard on in her face, she laughed, your ready then.

We had a great hour. I think she is the only escort that I have ever managed to get to orgasm, actually she came something like 5 times.

While I lived at this house I had two other escort ladies around.

The next one Wow, she was Wow. Words are hard to describe her.

Here I am 'mr average' with this absolute stunner next to me. She was not only extremely good looking, very good with people, wonderful to talk to. I hope she has made a fortune doing what she does, she deserves too.

Let me tell you just what she was like. After a guy cums, most of the time there is a quiet time, until he can get himself hard again. During this time we talked for a bit and she started to give me a hand massage. Oh wow.

Now I know that a hand massage is nothing to do with sex but as an erogenous experience when you have just had great sex with a really pretty lady, it is mighty good. Especially when you know you are going to do the same thing in a few minutes time.

I did break one of the golden rules that night. You should never ask an escort if she wants to be your boyfriend. She politely declined but she was such a wonderful person.

## Chapter Thirteen

## Ménage e trois

Or to put it another way, dinner for three.

I've done that twice so far, neither were exactly what I was looking for but here goes.

The first time was with a lady from a dating site. I think she did this a bit wrong, she was actually happily married, but they were missing something in their sex life.

To spice it up, what ever they were missing, they went out and got. They got what they were looking for and I got a shag so I don't suppose it all turned out so bad.

After chatting and finding out that yes she would meet for sex, but only accompanied by her husband.

Incidentally, the thing that they were missing was oral sex.

They had both been brought up to think of it as dirty so neither had ever experienced it.

We met in a pub, drove to my place and I started snogging her, boy could she snog well. I slid my hand inside her knickers and they were soaking.

Apparently she liked the look of me and the thought of what we were going to do and a great snog got her dripping.

Upstairs clothes off and as they were snogging away I got my head buried between her thighs. I was loving it. Her juices were flowing well and were very taisty. She was going from orgasm to orgasm and he was getting the snog of his life.

I did have a bit of a shag with her but yes, it was a little weird with her husband there. I think she had had a couple of kids by natural birth so things weren't to tight down there.

Apparently a few days later, as she had enjoyed the licking that I had given her so much that she final blew her husband.

Just before I left to work in Canada I had something that I wanted to do. I'd never been in a bedroom with two naked ladies.

There was a young escort that I had been to see a couple of times. Neither the sex nor the blow jobs were much to write home about but she was only young and that always made me feel good. There is also something good about visiting someone for sex that you have been with before.

Anyway. I'm messaged her to ask if she knew any other ladies that would double up with her. Yes, came the answer and her friend was the same price as she was that wasn't too bad.

There was one of the guys at work who I was always sharing stories with and I told him what I was up to. You lucky bastard was his response. Tell me about it afterwards.

This particular evening didn't work out quite right. I didn't get to see them on each other. I would loved to have fucked the pair of them while they were 69ing. Actually there are a lot of positions that I would love to do with two young ladies.

I did get to lick the pair of them and snuddle between them. It was nice but somewhat disappointing. Best I organise something better sometime soon.

## Chapter Fourteen

## Really!!!!!

I've has some really funny times like when I went to a 'massage parlour' not too far away from where I lived and all through the session I was having a laugh with this woman. She said 'your strange', I said 'I know'. Apparently most guys who went there just got on with it and barely spoke, I was cracking jokes and all sorts. It's actually really funny to get to the punchline of a joke just as she was taking my cock deep into her mouth. Ladies really do make a funny noise doing that.

Then there was the dating agency that I joined, I don't remember how much it cost but it was more than a couple of hundred pounds.

After a date I had to phone in and give my opinion of the date and of her. If the date went well according to both people then you just made your own arrangements. If it didn't, your opinions went to help finding other suitable matched from their records.

So I was describing to this lady how I liked a lady who could do more for her self, also one who was more up for it. 'I know what you mean'! I carried on chatting to her and realised that she was flirting with me.

The long and the short of it, I ended up shagging her every week for the next few weeks.

## Chapter Fifteen

## Greatest shags of my life

'Swallows a lot' was not only up for a good shagging at anytime. I used to have to tell her no more at 4 am, we'd been at it since 9 pm!

This ne night we were trying all sorts of positions and things. As there were just the two of us in the house we did it over the bath, on the stairs and in the kitchen. Over the dinning table and all over the sofa.

Then there was the garden.

We did it on the garden bench, on the grass. We were totally naked wandering around. Then we went into the garage and onto the motorbike. Oh such fun.

The last one I want to mention is the first shag with one of my girlfriends.

I was sat in a bar one Sunday night, the band had just finished, most of the people had left. I was just finishing off my beer before leaving and in she walks.

A quick snog and a look at that glint in here eye and I knew what she was after.

Oh boy did she have a good body. And tight, my got it nearly hurt to get my dick inside her. I was on top snogging her and pumping away when I started to have 'that feeling'.

Shit, I want to impress her the first time we do this.

Some how I managed to not cum, as she came in a shuddering orgasm I came gushing inside her. She said it was the best sex in her life.

So to end my horny tale, all of this is true, I love having great sex, shagging and making love.

Be happy and be safe, you know what I mean.

Ladies, feel free to contact me

RodgerABrown@gmail.om

Printed in Great Britain
by Amazon